HELPING YOUR BRAND-NEW READER

Here's how to make first-time reading easy and fun:

▶ Read the introduction at the beginning of each story aloud. Look through the pictures together so that your child can see what happens in the story before reading the words.

▶ Read the first page to your child, placing your finger under each word.

▶ Let your child touch the words and read the rest of the story. Give him or her time to figure out each new word.

▶ If your child gets stuck on a word, you might say, *"Try something. Look at the picture. What would make sense?"*

▶ If your child is still stuck, supply the right word. This will allow him or her to continue to read and enjoy the story. You might say, *"Could this word be 'ball'?"*

▶ Always praise your child. Praise what he or she reads correctly, and praise good tries too.

▶ Give your child lots of chances to read the story again and again. The more your child reads, the more confident he or she will become.

▶ Have fun!

First edition 2001

Library of Congress Cataloging-in-Publication Data

Ehrlich, Amy.
Kazam's magic / Amy Ehrlich ;
illustrated by Barney Saltzberg. — 1st ed.
p.   cm. — (Brand new readers)
Summary: Four stories about a young girl whose
magic tricks do not always turn out as she had hoped.
ISBN 0-7636-1309-6
[1. Magic tricks — Fiction.]
I. Saltzberg, Barney, ill. II. Title. III. Series.
PZ7.E328 Kaz 2001
[E] — dc21   00-065199

2 4 6 8 10 9 7 5 3 1

Printed in Hong Kong

This book was typeset in Letraset Arta.
The illustrations were done in watercolor and ink.

Candlewick Press
2067 Massachusetts Avenue
Cambridge, Massachusetts 02140

visit us at www.candlewick.com

KAZAM'S MAGIC

CANDLEWICK PRESS
CAMBRIDGE, MASSACHUSETTS

Amy Ehrlich ILLUSTRATED BY **Barney Saltzberg**

Contents

WHERE IS KAZAM?

Introduction

This story is called *Where Is Kazam?*
It is about what happens to her bird,
to her rabbit, and to Kazam when she
waves her wand.

Here is Kazam.

4

Here is Kazam's bird.

Here is Kazam's rabbit.

Here is Kazam's wand.

Kazam waves her wand.

Where is Kazam's bird?

Where is Kazam's rabbit?

Oops! Where is Kazam?

KAZAM'S COINS

11

Introduction

This story is called *Kazam's Coins.* It is about how Kazam waves her wand to make coins appear, then what Kazam does when a carrot appears instead.

13

Kazam has a coin.

14

Kazam waves her wand.

Kazam has two coins.

16

Kazam waves her wand again.

17

Kazam has three coins.

18

Kazam waves her wand again.

Kazam has a carrot.

Kazam throws her wand away.

KAZAM'S RABBIT

21

Introduction

This story is called *Kazam's Rabbit.* It is about how Kazam pulls a rabbit out of her hat, waves her wand, and poof! changes it to a frog, then poof! a mushroom, and then poof! back into a rabbit again. What does the rabbit do then?

Kazam pulls a rabbit out of her hat.

Kazam waves her wand.

25

Poof! Now it's a frog.

Kazam waves her wand.

Poof! Now it's a mushroom.

Kazam waves her wand.

29

Poof! Now it's a rabbit again.

The rabbit hops away.

KAZAM ALL WET

Introduction

This story is called *Kazam All Wet.*
It is about Kazam's magic trick in which
she puts a glass of water on her head
and waves her wand to make the glass
disappear. The water, however, does
not disappear.

Here is Kazam's glass.

Kazam puts water in her glass.

Kazam takes her hat off.

Kazam puts the glass on her head.

Kazam puts her hat on.

Kazam waves her wand.

Kazam takes her hat off.

Kazam is all wet!